To the little ones at
Ashland Christian Church

I hope this book helps you
feed your need to read!

Brian Rock

May '10

Don't Play With Your Food!

by Brian Rock

Illustrated by John Moerner

First Light Publishing
Richmond, VA

First Light Publishing
Richmond, VA

Printed in Canada

Library of Congress Control Number 2004092815
Rock, Brian. Don't Play With Your Food
Moerner, John. Illustrator
Summary: Collection of humorous food related poetry for children
ISBN 0-9754411-0-8

Dedicated to
Carter Christian Moerner
May you always dream of chocolate bunnies !
Love, Dad

It's fun to go bowling
At the old Salad Bowl.
The ball's made of lettuce,
So let us all roll

The ball down the alley
To the ten standing pins
Made of carrots and squash
Till somebody wins.

We'll knock down the veggie
Then we'll cheer as they fal
And when we have finished,
Tossed salad for all!

2

Betty Rosetti

Betty Rosetti has hair like spaghetti,
Spaghetti on top of her head.
Betty Rosetti has hair like spaghetti,
It's curly and swirly and red.

Betty Rosetti has hair like spaghetti,
She never eats out anywhere.
Betty Rosetti has hair like spaghetti,
She's scared that they'll eat up her hair!

SPUD LOVE

Spud was a tater
Lookin' for a mate or
Someone he could date or
Maybe just a friend.

Spud met Ida,
He took her for a ride-a
Through the countryside-a
And back home again.

Spud said "Baby,
Let's be wed today be-
Fore another day be-
Cause I love you lots!"

Spud and Ida
Moved to the west side-a
Where they now reside-a
Raising tater tots.

4

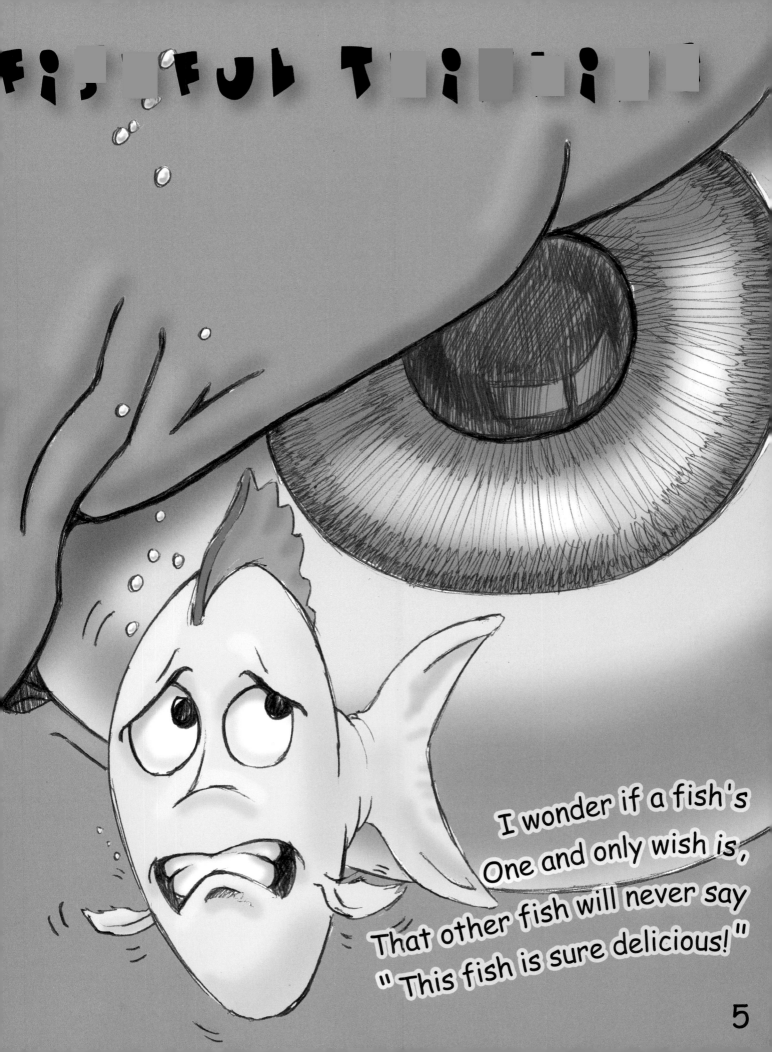

A Spicy Romance

Young salt and pepper
Went out to a dance,
Hoping to find
A spicy romance.

Salt danced with Green Bean
And Pepper with Ham,
But soon they switched partners
And danced once again.

Salt did the two step
And Pepper the twist,
Till each one had danced
With each guest on the list.

Then Salt looked at Pepper,
And Pepper at Salt.
They walked to each other
And came to a halt.

A new song was starting,
It played soft and light.
And Salt danced with Pepper
The rest of the night.

Just then the dance ended,
And time came to leave.
Then Salt reached around
And grabbed Pepper's sleeve.

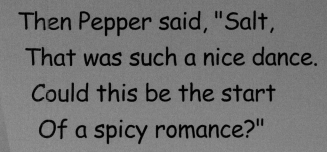

Then Pepper said, "Salt,
That was such a nice dance.
Could this be the start
Of a spicy romance?"

Salt said, "I hope so!"
And Salt wouldn't lie,
As the two stood there gazing
In each other's eyes.

Now they're happily married,
They couldn't want more;
And they still dance together
Behind cupboard doors!

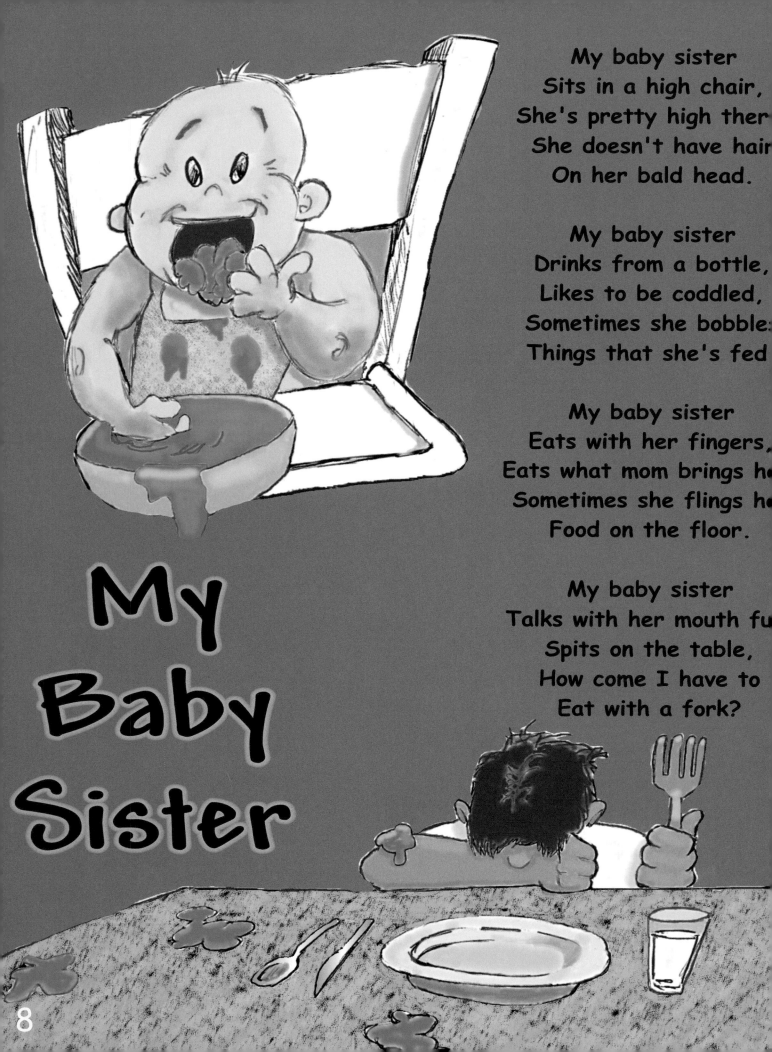

My baby sister
Sits in a high chair,
She's pretty high there,
She doesn't have hair
On her bald head.

My baby sister
Drinks from a bottle,
Likes to be coddled,
Sometimes she bobbles
Things that she's fed.

My baby sister
Eats with her fingers,
Eats what mom brings her,
Sometimes she flings her
Food on the floor.

My baby sister
Talks with her mouth full,
Spits on the table,
How come I have to
Eat with a fork?

My
Baby
Sister

Rita says her favorite food is squid.
Baloney I say!

Broccoli is the favorite food for Syd.
Baloney I say!

Kathy says she likes to eat some snails.
Baloney I say!

Kevin says he's eaten parts of whales.
Baloney I say!

Trina says she likes her carrots stewed.
Baloney I say!

If you want to know my favorite food.
Baloney I say!

Don't Eat With Your Fingers

Mom always says, "Don't eat with your fingers!"
I try to tell her I don't.
My friend says she can eat food with chopsticks.
I always tell her I won't.

Dad says up North they eat with utensils.
They eat with plain forks in the South.
But I only know one way of eating,
I only eat with my mouth!

11

Claire Eclair

Miss Claire Eclair
Was a beautiful pastry.
All covered with chocolate,
She looked very tasty

Filled with a cream
That just couldn't be sweeter;
Poor little Miss Eclair,
I just had to eat her!

MILK SHAKE

Farmer Brown has one strange cow
And Bessie is her name.
Ever since one day in June
She hasn't been the same.

On that day the ground did move.
The earth began to quake.
Now Bessie won't give normal milk,
She only gives milk shakes!

Kaboodles of Noodles

There's macaroni,
Rigatoni, angel hair,
And ravioli,
Tortelini and linguini,
Green and yellow fettucini,
Manicotti and rotini,
Regular and thin spaghetti,
Sea shell shaped and roteteli,
There's lasagna and elbow...
And those are all
The noodles I know!

CHEESEBURGER!

Cheeseburger, pleaseburger;
Can I have a cheeseburger?
I'll beg on my kneesburger
Just to get a cheeseburger!

Cheeseburger, weesburger;
Let's go get a cheeseburger!
Just a you and meesburger;
We can share a cheeseburger!

Cheeseburger, squeezeburger;
Please don't take my cheeseburger!
Don't you try to teaseburger;
Give me back my cheeseburger!

Cheeseburger, pleaseburger;
Can I have a cheeseburger?
I'll beg on my kneesburger
Just to get a cheeseburger!

Hotdog With Everything

Hotdog sitting on a bun,
Let's dress him up and have some fun:
A ketchup smile and mustard teeth,
A relish bow tie just beneath,
Some chili hair and onion eyes,
A hat of cheese
    piled way up high.
Hotdog sitting on a bun,
Now I can't see
    my hotdog none!

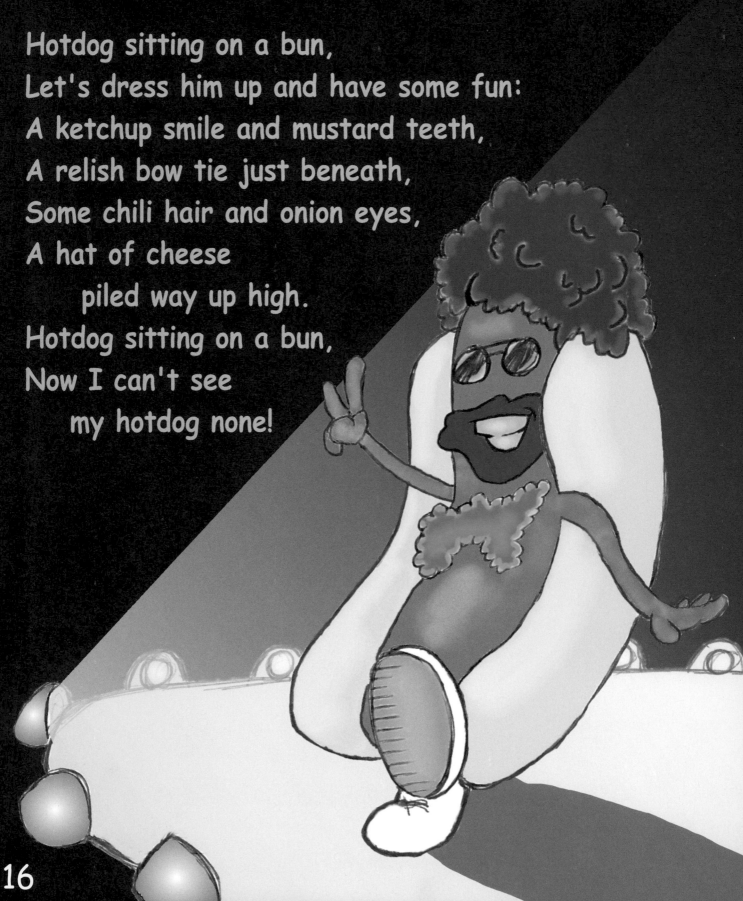

Watermelon

Watermelon, watermelon, green and white;
Watermelon, watermelon, what a sight!

You start from a seed planted in the ground;
You grow to weigh nearly forty pounds!

They pick you from the ground to feed us;
We eat your smile and spit your seed-uz!

Watermelon, watermelon, don't start yellin',
But I never liked to eat watermelon!

Ketchup for breakfast!
Ketchup for lunch!
And ketchup late at night!
    Ketchup makes me happy.
    It makes me feel all right.
Ketchup on pickles!
Ketchup on pears!
And ketchup on ice cream!
    Ketchup is delicious.
    It tastes just like a dream.
Ketchup on raisins!
Ketchup in milk!
And ketchup on my toast!
    Mom puts it on her french fries.
    I think that's really gross!

Tough Nut

Peanut Pete was awful rough,
Along with all his buddies.
He hardly ever acted right.
He never did his studies.

One day Pete a'salted nuts
Just standing on the corner.
Pete thought it was awful fun,
Till they called Sergeant Warner.

Sergeant Warner captured Pete.
He cornered him and shell'd him.
He took Pete to the local judge
Who sentenced Pete and cell'd him.

Peanut prison softened Pete,
Each passing day a little.
Now he's not so tough at all.
In fact, he's peanut brittle.

Food Fight

Down in the kitchen
One dreary, dark night,
I heard a strange sound
That didn't sound right.

I went to the kitchen
To investigate,
But when I arrived
I was already late.

Someone had blackened
All the peas' eyes.
They mashed the potatoes
And sliced up the pies.

They bruised the tomatoes
And whipped all the cream.
They cracked all the nuts
And made the ice scream.

The salad was tossed,
The butter was spread,
And lettuce was left
With only its head.

"Who could have done
Such a horrible thing?"
I said as I looked
At the whole messy scene.

An ear of corn said,
"I heard somebody walking!"
The onion cried out,
"I saw somebody stalking!"

"Aha!" I exclaimed.
I said "Thanks for the clue.
With this information
I know just what to do!"

I looked in the fridge,
On the bottom-most shelf;
And there sat the celery,
Alone, by itself.

The celery was covered
With bits of potato,
With whipped cream and butter,
And juice from tomatoes.

I asked why he did it.
He just wouldn't say.
So I picked up the celery
And threw him away.

The point of this story,
It's true, but it's sad...
It's not very pretty
When good food goes bad!

PB&J

Peanut butter
   and jelly
Is good my friends
   all tell me.
But when they eat
   that sandwich,
Their speech gets
   slightly damaged.
So instead of saying,
   'very good,"
They tell me that
   it's "bewy goob."

Peanut
Butter

GRAPE JELLY

Fruit Loops

Anna Banana
Went down to the fair,
Anna Banana
Saw papayas there.

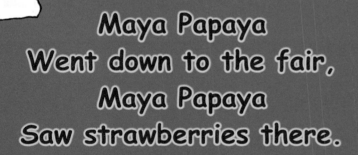

Maya Papaya
Went down to the fair,
Maya Papaya
Saw strawberries there.

Larry Strawberry
Went down to the fair,
Larry Strawberry
Saw bananas there...

23

Jambalaya

Boisenberries,
Girls in pie,
Mice in the cupboard,
Me oh my!

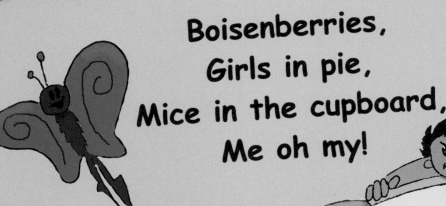

Almond pastry
She's in stew,
Bats in the belfr
Make them sho

Peanutbutter,
Butterfly,
Ants in the trousers,
Oh my my!

Jambalaya,
Lie about,
Bulls in the china,
Get them out!

Fruit Flies

Orange sprouted two new wings
And put them to good use,
Until he flew into a wall
And splattered orange juice.

Lemon grew a pair of wings
And flew in a parade,
But then she flew into a truck
And squeezed out lemonade.

Apple found a pair of wings
And flew to show his boss,
But on his way he hit a house
And turned to apple sauce.

So if you're going out to play
You better check the skies,
And take a coat or hat because
It's messy when fruit flies!

25

Hungry Hazards

There's a fly in my soup!
There is soup on my fly!
There's some juice in my grapefruit
That squirts in my eye!

There are peas in a sauce.
There is sauce on my nose!
There are carrots and broccoli
That someone else chose!

There is cheese on my meat.
There's now meat on my shirt!
There's no end to the hazards
To get to dessert!